RELAX

How to Manage Anxiety and Emotions in an Uncertain World

Barbara Diggs

ReferencePoint Press®

San Diego, CA

About the Author

Barbara Diggs is the author of multiple nonfiction books for middle-grade students. She lives in Paris, France, with her husband and two teenage sons.

© 2023 ReferencePoint Press, Inc.
Printed in the United States

For more information, contact:
ReferencePoint Press, Inc.
PO Box 27779
San Diego, CA 92198
www.ReferencePointPress.com

ALL RIGHTS RESERVED.
No part of this work covered by the copyright hereon may be reproduced or used in any form or by any means—graphic, electronic, or mechanical, including photocopying, recording, taping, web distribution, or information storage retrieval systems—without the written permission of the publisher.

LIBRARY OF CONGRESS CATALOGING-IN-PUBLICATION DATA

Names: Diggs, Barbara, author.
Title: Relax: Relax: How to Manage Anxiety and Emotions in an Uncertain World/ by Barbara Diggs.
Description: San Diego, CA : ReferencePoint Press, Inc., 2023. | Includes bibliographical references and index.
Identifiers: LCCN 2022043998 (print) | ISBN 978-1-6782-0482-2 (library binding) | ISBN 978-1-6782-0483-9 (ebook)
Subjects: LCSH: relaxation techniques--Juvenile literature. | Stress and anxiety in adolescence--Juvenile literature. | anxiety and relaxing in adolescence--Juvenile literature.

CONTENTS

Introduction   4
Youth in Distress

Chapter One   9
Recognizing Anxiety

Chapter Two   19
Get Grounded, Stay Connected

Chapter Three   30
Maintain a Healthy Lifestyle

Chapter Four   42
Healing Anxiety

Source Notes   54
Organizations and Websites   57
For Further Research   59
Index   61
Picture Credits   64

INTRODUCTION

Youth in Distress

For Brynn, the feelings of worthlessness started in her junior year of high school. Despite having good grades and playing in the school orchestra and on a varsity sports team, she was miserable. "I woke up every morning crying and dragged myself out of bed, feeling like I was carrying around a 50-pound backpack,"[1] she recalls.

She began to lose interest in everything—school, friends, even food—and started to have thoughts of harming herself. When she finally worked up the courage to discuss her feelings with her parents, her mother was insistent that she was only experiencing premenstrual syndrome. This reaction crushed Brynn's confidence and sent her into a downward mental spiral. She developed an eating disorder: restricting her meals to one per day, overexercising, and weighing herself constantly.

By Brynn's senior year, she began to experience anxiety attacks. But she ironically credits the attacks for having saved her life. Her parents took her symptoms more seriously after they saw her hyperventilating and shaking uncontrollably. They urged her to speak with the school guidance counselor.

Brynn sought help, but it was just the beginning of her mental health journey. She spent nearly three months of her senior year in the hospital and in different therapy programs for anxiety and depression. Her life began to improve once she found the right combination of therapy, medicine, and coping skills to reduce her symptoms. "If a friend or family member has talked to you about experiencing anything like this, know that they can get help," Brynn says. "I got through high school, and I am proud to be going to college next year."[2]

An Escalating Crisis

Brynn's experience is far from unique. Teens around the country have been experiencing anxiety and depression at surging rates. According to a study by the Centers for Disease Control and Prevention (CDC), the percentage of American high schoolers who say they feel persistent feelings of sadness or hopelessness rose from 26 percent in 2009 to 44 percent in 2021. Suicide rates among young people ages ten to twenty-four have leaped as well, increasing by a startling 60 percent between 2009 and 2018.

The COVID-19 pandemic only intensified the problem. Between March and October 2020, the percentage of emergency room visits for mental health crises rose by 31 percent among youth ages twelve to seventeen, according to the American Academy of Pediatrics' Healthy Children website. In early 2021, suspected suicide attempts among girls of that same age group also increased more than 50 percent compared to the same period in 2019.

The situation is so dire that in December 2021, the US surgeon general, Dr. Vivek Murthy, issued an official advisory to sound a public alarm about teens' deteriorating mental health and urge everyone to take the crisis seriously. The advisory emphasizes, "Mental health challenges in children, adolescents, and young adults are real, and they are widespread. . . . Our obligation to act is not just medical—it's moral."[3]

> "Mental health challenges in children, adolescents, and young adults are real, and they are widespread."[3]
>
> —Dr. Vivek Murthy, US surgeon general

Although the crisis is visible across all demographics, certain subsets of young people are especially at risk, including racial minorities, members of the LGBTQ+ community, immigrants, and youth who live in rural areas or in poverty. Black youth have had a

Experts believe that social media and technology play an important role in the skyrocketing rate of anxiety among teens.

particularly worrying increase in suicide rates. Between 2013 and 2019, suicides among Black males ages fifteen to twenty-four jumped by 47 percent and among females of the same age group by 59 percent.

What Is Behind It All?

It is no secret that adolescence is tough. Teens are grappling with their changing bodies, shifts in social relationships, and questions about their identities, all while dealing with the stresses of schoolwork and the uncertainty of looming adulthood. But these challenges are hardly new, so many wonder what accounts for the current surge in mental health challenges among teens.

There is no single answer. Mental health professionals largely agree that today's youth face an overwhelming number of stressful societal and global concerns. Gun violence, financial uncertainty, the effects of climate change, political divisiveness, and social and racial inequality are some of the major worries burdening youth. To all this, the COVID-19 pandemic added a pervasive sense of fear, anxiety, grief, and uncertainty. As thirteen-year-old Courtney Duffy put it when describing life as a modern teen to the New York Times, "I want to focus on school, on my artwork, on cross-country and track, on my friends, on my future. Instead, I'm left wondering if there will even be a future for my generation. . . . Coming of age in 2021 is realizing that the world is going up in flames, and you have to be the one to locate the fire extinguisher."[4]

Experts believe that social media and technology play important roles in the skyrocketing anxiety. "FOMO (fear of missing out), less face-to-face connection, pressures, bullying, news, violence, politics—it is all in the palm of a teen's hand on a daily basis for hours,"[5] says Sheryl Ziegler, a therapist and digital health adviser. Indeed, numerous studies have identified a link between social media and poor mental health. For example, psychologist Jean Twenge found that teens who are on social media for five or more hours a day, particularly girls, are twice as likely to be depressed as teens who do not use social media. Facebook, which owns Instagram, found that a third of teenage girls it surveyed reported that using Instagram makes them feel worse about their bodies.

> "Coming of age in 2021 is realizing that the world is going up in flames, and you have to be the one to locate the fire extinguisher."[4]
>
> —Courtney Duffy, a thirteen-year-old student

But it is not all bad news. Some mental health experts say that part of the rise in reports of anxiety and depression may be because young people are more open about their mental health struggles than earlier generations. Dr. Lynne Merk of Cincinnati Children's Hospital Medical Center says that modern society's greater awareness of mental health issues has led youth to be less judgmental about these issues than the older generation and more supportive of peers experiencing a crisis. This openness helps decrease stigma and makes it easier for young people to ask for help when needed.

What Can Be Done?

Parents, schools, and communities must work together to raise awareness of the crisis and find broad solutions for youth. But teens who are struggling with anxiety or other difficult emotions should be aware they are not alone with their feelings, and it is possible to get better. Countless teens have successfully learned coping skills, made lifestyle changes, or taken other proactive steps to help reduce or conquer their anxiety. Knowing how to manage anxiety makes it easier to weather challenging periods and to recognize that a feeling of wellness is achievable.

CHAPTER ONE

Recognizing Anxiety

When Christi Cazin was a teenager, she felt that something was wrong with her. She enjoyed hanging out with friends but hated being around large groups. She avoided class trips, birthday parties, and any situation that made her feel uncomfortable. The world seemed perpetually frightening and overwhelming, yet her friends and other people around her all seemed to be just fine.

Cazin did not realize that she was suffering from an anxiety disorder until she received a diagnosis as an adult. Now that she understands the root of her fearful feelings and has learned coping mechanisms, she feels as if she has been set free. "I still have moments where the world feels like it's sitting on my shoulders, but for the most part, it's *a lot* better. . . . Knowing what I'm up against has made it easier to handle."[6]

As Cazin's story shows, the first step to managing anxiety is knowing that you have it. But recognizing it is not always easy. "The fact is that anxiety exists at different levels and in different ways in each of us," writes *Harvard Business Review*

> "I still have moments where the world feels like it's sitting on my shoulders, but for the most part, it's *a lot* better. . . . Knowing what I'm up against has made it easier to handle."[6]
>
> —Christi Cazin, an anxiety sufferer

> "The fact is that anxiety exists at different levels and in different ways in each of us. There's no one-size-fits-all."[7]
>
> —Charlotte Lieberman, *Harvard Business Review* author

author Charlotte Lieberman, who has struggled with anxiety since childhood. "There's no one-size-fits-all."[7]

Learning as much as possible about anxiety can help you identify the symptoms in yourself and others and understand when it is time to seek help.

What Is Anxiety?

Anxiety is a feeling of fear or unease that arises in response to stress. When we detect danger or stress, the brain immediately sends an alert to the rest of the body through the nervous system. The nervous system then triggers a fight-or-flight response, urging the body to either run or fight the danger. Anxiety is part of the body's warning system. These feelings tell us that danger is nearby and that we need to react to protect ourselves.

Our prehistoric ancestors needed anxiety and the fight-or-flight response to react quickly to the major stressors in their lives: dangerous wild animals or threatening strangers. Today, our major daily stressors have changed somewhat. We still experience anxiety when we sense a physical threat but also when there is a psychological one. In modern life, you might recognize anxiety as the feeling of butterflies in your stomach before taking an important exam or the way your heart starts pounding when asking someone out on a date.

Having some anxiety is normal and even useful. It can make you more focused and help you prepare for a difficult or uncertain situation. For instance, if you have an upcoming piano recital, your anxiety about performing in front of a crowd might motivate you to practice more. If you are walking alone on a dark street, anxiety makes you more alert to unusual noises or movements, and it prepares your body to react if you feel threatened.

Anxiety becomes problematic when it spins out of control. An anxiety disorder arises when the brain keeps signaling danger in situations in which there is no threat. When this occurs, you feel fearful or worried almost all the time, usually to the point that it disrupts your life and you have trouble functioning normally.

Several types of anxiety disorders exist. Generalized anxiety disorder (GAD) is one of the most common. A person with GAD feels chronic, extreme worry and tension about anything and everything without cause. People with social anxiety disorder feel intense anxiety, self-consciousness, and fear of judgment in social situations. Someone with obsessive-compulsive disorder has recurrent, obsessive thoughts and worries and engages in repetitive behaviors in hopes of getting rid of those thoughts. Other anxiety disorders include panic disorders, separation anxiety disorder, and phobias. According to the National Institute for Mental Health, approximately 31.9 percent of teens suffer from an anxiety disorder.

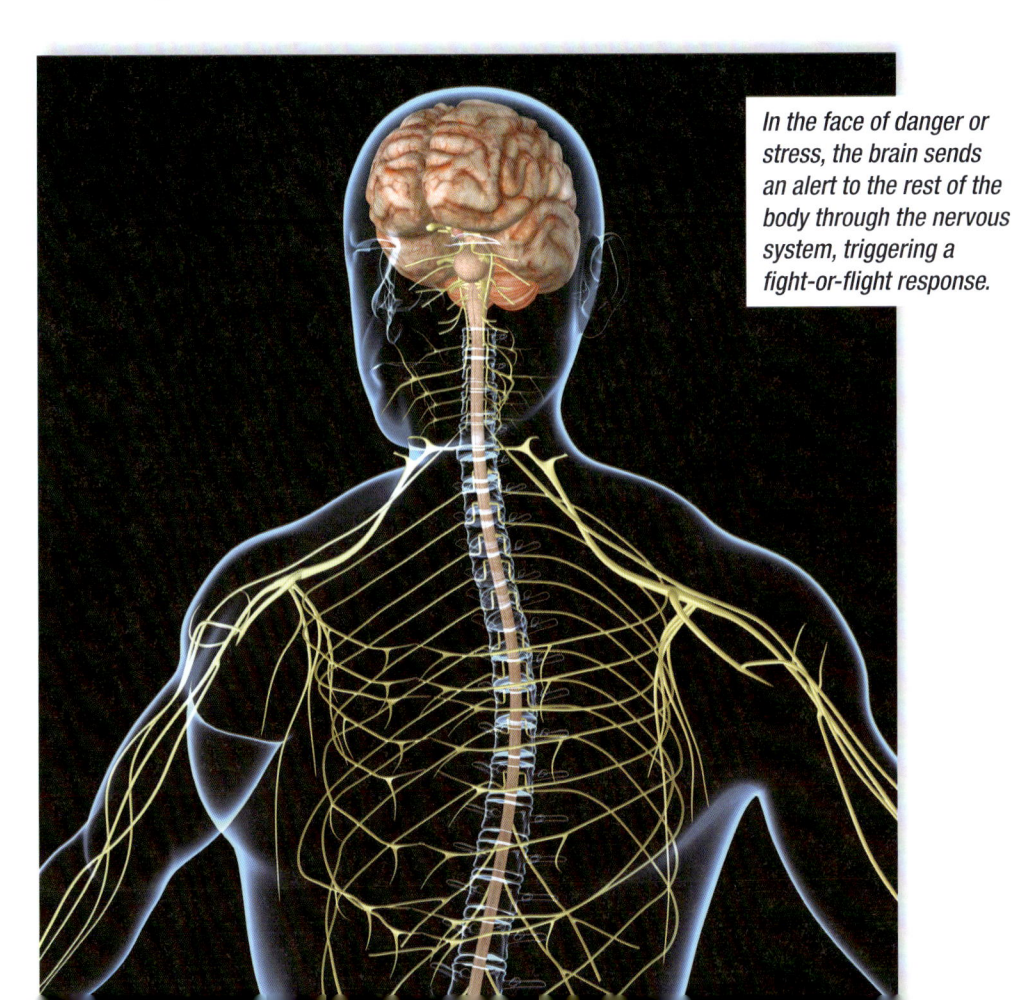

In the face of danger or stress, the brain sends an alert to the rest of the body through the nervous system, triggering a fight-or-flight response.

Symptoms of Anxiety

Anxiety symptoms differ from person to person. For Charlotte Lieberman, it took the form of the compulsion to clean. At age nine, Lieberman's parents found her repeatedly scrubbing their bathroom. She would organize their medicine cabinet according to color and size and toss out expired medicines. In particular, she loved washing the sink because she could feel her fears and troubles spiraling down the drain along with the dirty water.

More commonly, people tend to experience anxiety through physical symptoms. Anxiety can affect your body in a range of surprising and unsettling ways. Headaches, stomachaches, sweating, trembling, dizziness, hyperventilating, shortness of breath, restlessness, and an accelerated heart rate are some of the usual signs.

Some people experience several physical symptoms all at once, along with a powerful sense of dread and fear. This phenomenon is known as a panic attack. Panic attacks often arise without warning and usually last for ten to twenty minutes. Although they are treatable and not inherently dangerous, they can be terrifying, especially when you do not understand what is happening to you. Tyler Ellis, who was sixteen when he experienced his first panic attack, thought he was having a heart attack:

> My very first panic attack snuck up on me out of the blue. I was standing in my parents' bedroom, talking to my mother. . . . Suddenly, my heart and mind were racing beyond any semblance of control. My breathing soon followed—I felt like a fish out of water, desperately gasping for oxygen yet feeling like somehow there wasn't enough in the room. . . . I quickly walked out of my parents' room and into the living room. . . . Within a few minutes I was lying on the couch, fully convinced that I was going to die.[8]

Anxiety can impact your mind as much as your body. Psychological symptoms include having hard-to-shake worrying thoughts or beliefs, difficulty concentrating, and forgetfulness. It

Different Meanings

Worry, *stress*, and *anxiety* are terms we often use interchangeably, yet they are distinct emotional states.

"Worry is what happens when your mind dwells on negative thoughts, uncertain outcomes, or things that could go wrong," explains psychologist Melanie Greenberg. "It's the cognitive component of anxiety." You may feel unhappy or frightened while worried, but the feelings do not trigger a bodily reaction. Worry usually spurs you to find solutions to the problems troubling you.

Stress occurs when you have a fight-or-flight response (a pounding heart, faster breathing, bodily tension, or hyperalertness) to a recognized threat. You may feel stress when facing a challenging or uncertain situation, such as just before a college interview or while playing a high-stakes basketball game. Once the threat ends, the feelings fade.

Anxiety is when you have a fight-or-flight response to an unrecognizable threat. You are likely feeling anxiety if you feel physical stress or worry for no apparent reason, or in response to a nonthreatening stimulus, such as an empty classroom. "Anxiety is what happens when you're dealing with a lot of worry and a lot of stress," says Dr. Luana Marques. Finding ways to reduce worry and stress could help prevent anxiety.

Quoted in Emma Pattee, "The Difference Between Worry, Stress, and Anxiety," *New York Times*, February 26, 2020. www.nytimes.com.

---

is not unusual for anxious adolescents to see their grades take a nosedive or become wildly inconsistent as they struggle to stay focused on school matters, in the classroom or outside of it. In other teens, anxiety may manifest as excessive worry about assignments and grades. They fret over every small task, so they study until they are ready to—and sometimes do—collapse with overwhelming exhaustion.

Emotional and behavioral changes can also indicate anxiety. You might feel constantly fatigued, inexplicably irritable and angry, or get frustrated easily. Suddenly, you have less interest in doing things with your friends or participating in your favorite activities, preferring instead to stay in your room or in bed to be alone with your thoughts. However, mental health professionals say the more time you spend on your own with anxious thoughts, the greater your anxiety is likely to grow.

The Dangers of Untreated Anxiety

The good news is that anxiety can be successfully treated. It can take time to find the right combination of therapy, lifestyle changes, and perhaps medication, but many teens who struggle with anxiety can move forward to live happy, productive lives. Unfortunately, less than half the young people who need treatment for anxiety receive care, according to a 2020 report by the *Journal of the American Academy of Child and Adolescent Psychiatry*. Left untreated, teens are at risk of developing serious problems that will make their lives much more complicated.

An untreated anxiety disorder can have a serious impact on your health. When you experience anxiety, cortisol and adrenaline flood your body. These stress hormones give you the boost of energy you need in fight-or-flight situations. However, when your body repeatedly produces adrenaline or cortisol over the long term, you can suffer a range of physical effects, including immune system deficiencies, weight gain, high blood pressure, and heart

Some anxious teens try to self-medicate by using drugs or alcohol, but the use of such substances carries more risk than many young people realize.

Anxiety Triggers: What You Should Know

An anxiety trigger is a specific situation or action that activates the fight-or-flight response and makes a person feel fearful or worried. Triggers are deeply personal to each individual and can come from a range of internal or external sources.

External triggers might include an upcoming school exam, social gatherings, conflict or bullying, lack of money, news reports, violence, illness, or even caffeine, unhealthy foods, or insufficient sleep. Internal anxiety triggers are those that come from inside your own mind. These might include a demanding desire for perfection, lack of control over a situation, having low confidence or self-esteem, or feeling persistent shame, guilt, or embarrassment over a situation or incident that occurred in the past.

"Half the battle of challenging our anxiety is knowing how to recognize when it is happening," says therapist Carissa Weber. "Taking time during your day to do an emotional check-in with yourself to identify both the physical and emotional feelings you are having is a great start to learning about your anxiety." Once you understand your triggers, you can use coping techniques before or during anxiety-provoking situations to prevent anxiety from taking over.

Carissa Weber, "What Anxiety Really Is: A Map of Distress to Nowhere," *That Darn Amygdala* (blog), April 21, 2021. https://thatdarnamygdala.com.

---

disease. High amounts of these hormones can also worsen your anxiety and put you at increased risk for developing other mental conditions, such as depression or panic disorder.

Leaving anxiety untreated also puts you at risk of turning to harmful coping mechanisms. Some anxious teens try to self-medicate by turning to unhealthy or illegal substances to feel calmer and more able to cope with their anxieties. "I've had very stressed-out kids say, 'I get high before I go to school because I'm so anxious when I think about the start of the school day,'" says Jeannette Friedman, a social worker who works with families of adolescents with substance use problems. "[They say,] 'If I smoke a little weed, I don't feel so anxious.'"[9]

The occasional puff of marijuana or bottle of beer carries more risk than many teens may realize. Teens become addicted to alcohol or drugs much faster than adults. The prefrontal cortex, the part of the brain that regulates self-control and rationality, does not fully develop until the mid-twenties. Yet the reward center of the brain, which drives us to repeat pleasurable behaviors, is already well developed by adolescence. This means that some teens may have a strong impulse to use drugs or alcohol but do not have the capacity to put the brakes on high-risk behavior.

Restrictive eating and bingeing and purging are other common, detrimental ways some anxious teens cope with their emotions. Dr. Amelia Davis, who is director of Rosewood Ranch, an eating disorder clinic in Arizona, says about 50 percent of people with eating disorders had an anxiety disorder prior to developing unhealthy eating habits. Many teens develop eating disorders because deciding how to eat gives them a sense of control that they do not have anywhere else in their lives. But while this feeling of control may relieve anxiety in the moment, eating disorders can cause numerous other serious health problems, including damage to the heart, digestive system, bones, and teeth. If left uncontrolled, it may even cause malnutrition and death. Although eating disorders are primarily associated with girls, about one in three boys and men develop eating disorders as well.

Anxiety and Self-Harm

It is becoming increasingly common for some anxious teens to injure or inflict pain on themselves to find relief. "It makes the world very quiet for a few seconds," admits Faith-Ann, who often cut her arms and torso as a teen to relieve her anxiety. "For a while I didn't want to stop, because it was my only coping mechanism. I hadn't learned any other way."[10] Self-harm can take a range of forms, including cutting, burning, pulling out hair, piercing one's skin with a sharp object, banging one's head, or exercising to the point of collapse.

A 2018 survey of sixty-five thousand US high school students showed that approximately 18 percent of the students—one out of four girls and one out of ten boys—have engaged in at least one act of self-harm. This rate appears to have dramatically increased during the COVID-19 pandemic. FAIR Health's 2021 survey of medical records and insurance claims revealed that claims for intentional self-harm among teens between thirteen and eighteen increased 99.8 percent between 2019 and 2020.

Most teens who engage in self-harm are not looking to kill themselves: they are seeking a temporary release from their anxiety symptoms. However, there is no denying that some self-harming teens do end their lives. Teen suicide is now the second-leading cause of death among twelve- to seventeen-year-olds in the United States, according to pediatric emergency room records. What is more, teens who suffer from anxiety or depression are at higher risk of considering or committing suicide. These worrying facts make it even more important for anxious teens to seek help for this treatable condition.

Asking for Help

One of the more frustrating aspects of anxiety is that people unfamiliar with the condition can fail to recognize or misinterpret the symptoms. Uninformed teachers may think of an anxious teen as

One way to ease the fear of talking to a parent is to ask your parent to take a walk with you. The act of walking and talking can make it easier to explain complicated feelings and also to ask for help.

being deliberately defiant, attention seeking, or lazy. Parents may brush off their teen's feelings as a normal part of adolescence or think they are being oversensitive. However, if your anxiety feels out of control, it is essential to ask for help from an adult, even if you fear you will not be taken seriously.

Psychotherapist Katie Hurley suggests approaching your parents during a low-key moment, when they are not busy or stressed. She also recommends raising the topic while engaged in another relaxing or hands-on activity with them. "Taking a walk together is a good way to open up when you feel ready," says Hurley. "Sometimes it's easier to open up when you're not staring right at your parents seeing their facial expressions as you talk."[11]

When talking to your parents, focus on describing how you feel and specifically asking for help to manage your feelings. For example, you might tell them that you dread school so much it makes you feel panicky, shaky, and sick. Emphasize that these feelings are not just normal bouts of anxiety but a large problem that you need help managing. Hurley suggests creating a list of your symptoms beforehand that you can refer to during your conversation.

If your parents do not take you seriously the first time you speak to them about your anxiety, do not give up. Consider showing them articles or YouTube videos about anxiety so that they can understand it better. Also consider speaking to another trusted adult in your life, such as a school counselor, teacher, coach, or an aunt or uncle. They may be able to convince your parents of the urgency of the situation or otherwise help you find the support you need.

If you are experiencing an immediate mental health crisis and fear you might hurt yourself, call the 988 Suicide and Crisis Lifeline; 988 is the new three-digit dialing code that will route callers to the National Suicide Prevention Lifeline. These resources are available to help you twenty-four hours a day, seven days a week.

CHAPTER TWO

Get Grounded, Stay Connected

For a long time, sixteen-year-old Kerry felt trapped in her own mind by anxiety. During an anxious moment or panic attack, her thoughts started racing and she felt disconnected from the people around her. "It can feel like I'm stuck in slow motion, or that everything is in fast forward. . . . Sometimes I try to talk, but can feel my voice running away from me, or my words. Before I know it, the whole world feels as though it has fallen into chaos, and yet I'm the only one who's noticed."[12]

Although anxiety feels different for everyone, having spiraling, out-of-control thoughts and feeling disconnected from others are common features. The key to breaking free of anxiety's grip lies in grounding yourself to the present moment. Though you may not realize it, when experiencing anxiety, your mind is not in the here and now. It is busy anticipating negative events (*What if I fail this test and never get into college*?) or dwelling on negative perceptions or happenings in the past (*I made a fool of myself when I was at Jake's party last month*).

Grounding is the act of diverting your attention away from negative thoughts and concentrating on things happening around you. By anchoring your thoughts to the present, your mind and body begin to understand that there is no current threat, and they can relax their vigilance. To achieve this present-centered state, known as mindfulness, it is good to have a variety of grounding techniques at your disposal.

Deep Breathing

A grounding technique can be anything that draws your attention to the present. It might be doing something that reconnects you to your body, surroundings, senses, or other people. Although numerous grounding methods exist, for many mental health experts, deep breathing tops the list.

People have used deep breathing to calm down since ancient times. The method works because taking slow, deep breaths soothes the sympathetic nervous system, which is the system that kicks us into fight-or-flight mode. At the same time, deep breathing stimulates the parasympathetic nervous system, which is responsible for slowing our heart rate and relaxing our body. Molly, seventeen, who suffered from debilitating anxiety attacks, was surprised at how well deep breathing helped her: "When people used to tell me to breathe when having an attack, I would ignore it as I couldn't imagine that something as simple as breathing could have such an impact! I was wrong. Today, I rely on breathing to control my anxiety."[13]

Box breathing (also called square breathing) is a well-known technique used by therapists, yoga teachers, and US Navy Sea, Air, and Land (SEAL) teams alike to elicit calm. To use this technique, breathe slowly and deeply through your nose for four seconds, hold your breath for four seconds, exhale through your mouth for four seconds, then hold your breath again for four seconds. Continue this pattern until you feel calmer and more in touch with your body. If four seconds feels too long, try using two or three seconds instead, as long as you keep the timing of each phase equal.

The belly breathing technique is another popular method. Sit in a chair or lie down with a pillow under your head. Place one hand on your chest and the

> "When people used to tell me to breathe when having an attack, I would ignore it as I couldn't imagine that something as simple as breathing could have such an impact! I was wrong. Today, I rely on breathing to control my anxiety."[13]
>
> —Molly, a seventeen-year-old student

Deep breathing is a well-known technique for diverting attention from negative thoughts and concentrating on what is going on around you.

other on your belly, just below the rib cage. Inhale through your nose slowly and visualize the air moving downward, pushing your belly outward. Next, exhale slowly and fully through slightly pursed lips as your belly deflates. Continue until your anxiety recedes.

To enhance your sense of calm, try surrounding yourself with the scent of lavender while performing your deep breathing exercise. Lavender contains a fragrant chemical called linalool that has been clinically shown to help relieve anxiety. Use an aromatherapy diffuser, an essential oil spray, or a lavender-scented candle to disperse the scent.

Getting Present in Your Body

Anxiety can sometimes produce a strange out-of-body sensation. During these moments, it may feel as if your mind is in a fog or trapped by your thoughts. In more extreme cases, you may experience depersonalization, a condition in which it feels as if you, or nothing around you, is real. When your mind feels separate from your body, sensorial grounding techniques can help reconnect the two.

Experts say that one of the quickest ways to return to your body is to make intentional bodily contact with the ground. If possible, go outside to stand in grass or dirt with your bare feet. If you cannot do that, standing on a tile floor or carpet with bare feet can also work. When using this technique, concentrate on the sensations you feel: Is the ground hard, rocky, or soft? Does it tickle the bottom of your feet, or is it smooth? Is the tile cold or warm? How does it feel when you wiggle your toes or when you rub your feet on the ground?

If you seek a more stimulating sensation, an ice cube can help. Dr. Julie Smith went viral on TikTok in 2020 when she showed several different hacks for reducing anxiety and getting grounded with ice. Among other things, she suggested holding the cube in your hand while focusing on its temperature and texture, sliding it up and down your arm, or even sticking your face in a bowl of ice water. The coldness can shift your mind away from anxious thoughts or mental fogginess and make you feel more present as you pay attention to the discomfort of the ice on your skin.

Other recommended ways to reconnect to your body include biting into a lemon, savoring a favorite scent, or doing simple exercises, such as a few jumping jacks or stretches. Whatever you choose, the most important thing is to concentrate on the bodily sensations these actions produce.

Labeling Exercises

Some teens find mindfulness exercises particularly helpful in shifting their attention away from anxious thoughts. This simple technique involves looking around and consciously naming or labeling objects around you until you are calmer. You can add another layer to the exercise by naming aloud items only of a specific color. For example, in your bedroom, you might say, "I see a yellow folder; I see a yellow pillowcase; I see a yellow sock." When you exhaust the first color, switch to a different one.

The Power of Pets

Spending time with a beloved pet or another friendly animal can bring numerous emotional benefits, including lowering anxiety and boosting your mood. "Petting, holding, or cuddling an animal increases the levels of serotonin and dopamine in our bodies, which are feeling good calming brain chemicals," explains Dr. Louise Miller in *Psychology Today*. Pets can also give you much-needed affection and attention and provide a supportive, nonjudgmental ear. Although dogs and cats are particularly well known as emotional support animals, other animals, even nonfurry ones, can also provide positive benefits. A study published in *Environment and Behavior* found that watching fish swim for just ten minutes can lower blood pressure and make people feel happier and more relaxed.

If you do not have a pet or are not able to have one, you can still benefit from animal love by volunteering at your local animal shelter. Most shelters constantly need volunteers to comfort and care for the animals. As a volunteer, you will not only reap the positive emotional benefits of being around animals but also feel good knowing you are making homeless animals feel loved too.

Louise B. Miller, "The Psychological and Physical Benefits of Having a Pet," *Mind Body Connection* (blog), *Psychology Today*, October 26, 2020. www.psychologytoday.com.

The 5-4-3-2-1 grounding technique combines labeling and sensory awareness. Start by identifying five things you can see around you. Next, name four things you can feel in the moment, whether an emotional or physical sensation. Then, pick three things you can hear, two things you can smell, and one taste you detect. If you do not have certain senses, complete the 5-4-3 exercises with the senses that you do have, then identify two things that make you happy and one thing that is great about you.

Kerry says the alphabet game has been the most effective labeling technique for her. In this exercise, you pick a category—animals, countries, foods—then name something for every letter of the alphabet within that category. "This isn't an instant fix by any means," she says, "but it's an excellent grounding technique to get your brain switched back from the fear and panic that has thrown all rationality out the window."[14]

Pop on Your Playlist

When wrapped in anxiety, it can feel like you will never feel happy or at ease again. But your favorite music can help loosen anxiety's hold. Many studies have found that listening to music—or playing a musical instrument—can calm your nervous system, decrease anxiety, and lower stress. These benefits are likely to occur for multiple reasons.

First, when we listen to music, our brain releases a neurotransmitter called dopamine, a chemical that activates our brain's pleasure and reward center. This rush of dopamine almost immediately makes us feel good. "[Music] offers an easy distraction or diversion," says music therapist Tim Ringgold. "Since music triggers a pleasure response, our brain is all too happy to focus on a music signal to the exclusion of anything else."[15]

What is more, music has a significant physiological effect on our bodies. Listening to relaxing music can lower your heart rate, deepen your breathing, and decrease the level of stress hormones in your body, says Indre Viskontas, author of the book *How Music Can Make You Better*. This effect occurs because your brain

Many studies have found that listening to music can calm your nervous system, decrease anxiety, and lower stress.

tries to sync with the music. When the music has a slower beat, parts of the autonomic nervous system slow as well. Music is so effective at reducing anxiety that several studies have found that patients who listened to music before surgery need fewer anxiety-reducing sedatives than patients who did not.

Music also offers an excellent method of grounding yourself to the present. Dancing, clapping, snapping your fingers, or just tapping your feet along to your favorite tunes can turn your mind toward your body's movements and the rhythm of the music instead of an anxious loop of thoughts.

Take a Digital Detox

Many teens do not like to hear it, but the amount of time spent online might contribute to higher anxiety. The internet is rife with anxiety-inducing content, whether you are seeing image after image of other people's seemingly perfect lives or being inundated with articles about political tensions. Because internet algorithms are designed to keep you gazing at such content for as long as possible, it is easy for viewers to become worried or depressed.

A 2019 study published in *JAMA Psychiatry* found that teens who spend more than three hours online experience more anxiety and depression than those who do not. And most teens are spending far more than three hours online. Common Sense Media reports that in 2021 teens spent an average of eight hours and thirty-nine minutes per day online. Although this figure may be due to the pandemic's quarantine restrictions, even the prepandemic screen-time figures of seven hours and twenty-two minutes per day worry mental health experts. Spending long hours alone and online can exacerbate the symptoms of social anxiety, depression, or other mental health issues.

Taking a break from social media, gaming, or general screen use, therefore, can improve anxiety symptoms. A study published in *Cyberpsychology, Behaviour and Social Networking* in 2022 showed that taking just a one-week break from social media

Meditation Reduces Anxiety

Meditation is an ancient practice intended to help a person obtain mental clarity and a heightened state of awareness. It also reduces anxiety's physical and mental symptoms, as a growing body of research shows. Although many types of meditation exist, almost all forms involve centering your focus on an object, action, or word for a set period and allowing any other thoughts to pass through your mind without judgment.

Try sitting in a quiet space and focusing on the word *peace* for ten minutes, either repeating it aloud or in your head. When anxious thoughts intrude, acknowledge and accept them, but then return your mind to the word *peace*. With consistent practice, your mind will likely grow calmer, and you can carry this sense of calm even when not meditating.

"Since I've been meditating, I've noticed that I'm more relaxed and I face problems a little bit differently than I might have," says sixteen-year-old Chloe Ashton. "I look at them with more of an open mind, but I've also only been meditating for a couple weeks. I'm excited to see the changes in the future."

Quoted in Dan Harris, "Meditation Becoming More Popular Among Teens." ABC News, January 2, 2015. https://abcnews.go.com.

---

significantly reduced individuals' symptoms of anxiety and depression and improved their overall level of well-being. Similarly, a survey by the organization Game Quitters found that many gamers who reported taking a ninety-day break from gaming felt more optimistic, more psychologically healthy, and had improved performances at school or work.

Gathering the willpower to break from your favorite digital activities can be tough. But there are ways to make it easier. Start by setting a small goal. Challenge yourself to stay offline for a short period, such as nights or during mealtimes, for one or two weeks. If you are feeling ambitious, aim for a twenty-four-, forty-eight-, or seventy-two-hour break. If a particular app or two is draining your time and energy, delete those apps for a specific period.

Next, create a list of things you would like to do or accomplish during your newly free offline time. It does not have to be anything elaborate. If you are used to scrolling into the wee hours of the night, you might want to catch up on sleep. Or you might decide to learn to cook something new, read a book, see a movie with a good friend, or play your favorite sport. Knowing that you will benefit from offline time in some way can help keep you motivated.

Avoid temptation by turning off those push notifications that sound every time an app wants to claim your attention. These notifications interrupt your real-world experiences to pull you back into the digital world. It may also help to enlist the aid of your parents or a trusted friend by asking them to hang on to your phone during offline periods. Alternatively, consider setting screen-time limits on your phone that temporarily block you from the internet.

Keeping a detox journal will help you better observe the results of your efforts. Every day, write down how much time you spent online, the activities you engaged in when offline, and your general anxiety levels. When online, did you find your anxiety increasing when visiting certain sites or following specific people or threads? Have you noticed a pattern of feeling less anxious after a period of detox? These observations can help you understand whether or how your anxiety is connected to being online and allow you to make the appropriate adjustments.

Name It to Tame It

Sometimes just talking about difficult feelings can ease anxiety and help ground you. Strong emotions are rooted in a tiny structure in our brain called the amygdala. When an anxiety-provoking event occurs, it is the amygdala that reacts, setting off a chain reaction of neural impulses that send the body into fight-or-flight mode.

But scientists have found that talking about negative emotions diminishes the amygdala's response. The sense of threat recedes, and the body relaxes. "[Venting] helps take the feelings out from inside of yourself, it helps you to process them," says

Learning to cook something new is a good way to use spare time that was previously devoted to digital activities.

Eva Stubits, a Houston-based clinical psychologist. "It's kind of like the pressure cooker analogy: If you don't open a lid periodically, the steam can build up and cause you to feel even more stressed. If you let it out, it can help you process whatever it is you're worried about."[16]

Talking to someone about your anxieties can also help you feel less alone. Express your feelings to someone you trust, whether a good friend, your parents, teacher, coach, guidance counselor, or a community member. You might also ask your parents to help you find an anxiety support group, either online or in person. Many teens are surprised and relieved to realize how many peers ex-

> "[Venting] helps take the feelings out from inside of yourself, it helps you to process them."[16]
>
> —Eva Stubits, a clinical psychologist

perience the same anxious or depressed feelings as they do and how good it feels to share.

If no one is available to talk during an anxious moment, try simply naming your emotions. Psychologist Dan Siegel of the University of California, Los Angeles, conducted a study that found that just saying negative emotions aloud can put distance between you and your feelings, making your reaction to them less intense. Siegel theorizes that such labeling diminishes the reactive response of the amygdala and allows more rational parts of the brain to take over. The next time you feel anxious, say "I am anxious" or "This is anxiety," and lean into this understanding. Like other grounding techniques, naming your emotions can help bring you into the present moment and break the power of a negative emotional spiral.

CHAPTER THREE

Maintain a Healthy Lifestyle

As teen anxiety and mental disorders escalate, more health professionals are calling on the public to pay greater attention to the link between physical and mental health. Physical health can have a profound impact on psychological health and vice versa.

Maintaining a healthy, balanced lifestyle is essential for better physical and mental health and reduced anxiety and stress. The core elements of healthy living include engaging in regular exercise, eating nutrient-rich foods, and getting ample amounts of sleep. Unfortunately, many teens do not follow routines that maintain these healthy requirements.

Healthy Body, Healthier Mind

Fifteen-year-old Ben Morris did not like leaving the house, rarely spoke to people outside his close group of friends, and found it difficult to cope with the stresses of puberty. But his life changed after his doctor prescribed exercise to treat his anxiety. He began to work with a trainer and work out consistently. "There's quite a big period after exercise where I feel quite at peace and quite content with life," says Ben. "As I exercise, I'm able to become more happy and confident in myself."[17]

Experts have long known that exercise has a positive effect on mental health. Moderate or vigorous exercise stimulates the production of endorphins, a brain chemical that makes you feel good—even euphoric—and reduces the perception of pain. Exercise also reduces the body's levels of stress hormones, helps distract you from anxious or negative thoughts, and promotes better sleep. It can even boost self-confidence as it improves your physical and mental strength.

> "As I exercise, I'm able to become more happy and confident in myself."[17]
>
> —Ben Morris, a fifteen-year-old student with anxiety

The CDC recommends that children between the ages of six and seventeen exercise at least sixty minutes daily. However, a survey conducted by the University of Georgia in 2022 found that 75 percent of US teens, particularly girls, are not hitting these targets. This lack of activity is concerning, especially in light of a 2019 survey of thirty-five thousand youth that showed that children who do not exercise are twice as likely to have anxiety, depression, or other mental health problems compared to children who met exercise goals.

Anxiety-Busting Activities

You do not have to run a marathon to obtain the mental benefits of exercise; even modest physical activity can positively affect your emotional state. "Moderate activity of any kind, getting out and doing something, is associated with improvements, lower levels of depressive symptoms, lower levels of anxiety, better well-being,"[18] says Elaine McMahon, a research fellow at the National Suicide Research Foundation and the School of Public Health at University College Cork, Ireland. The most important thing is doing physical activities that you enjoy.

Nearly every form of physical activity can boost mental health, so your options are wide open. Shooting hoops, playing soccer, swimming, skateboarding, walking your dog, dancing to YouTube videos, gardening, or playing an instrument are all physical activities that can provide a mental lift. If you are crunched for time or are not sporty, start small: commit to taking a twenty-minute walk every day, doing ten jumping jacks or side stretches after finishing each homework assignment, or taking the stairs instead of using an elevator.

You may want to try activities specifically known for their anxiety-reducing potential. Yoga is a gentle form of exercise long associated with anxiety and stress reduction—a viewpoint increasingly supported by clinical research. Researchers believe yoga's emphasis on mindful movements and breathing techniques stimulates the brain stem's vagus nerve, which helps calm the fight-or-flight response of the sympathetic nervous system. Studies have also found that yoga increases the brain's levels of gamma-aminobutyric acid (GABA). GABA is a neurotransmitter known for calming anxiety and stress.

Health care professionals are increasingly suggesting yoga as a complementary treatment for teens with anxiety. In addition to its mental benefits, yoga is noncompetitive and open to all ability levels, promotes self-acceptance, and can be practiced at home. Even a few simple yoga stretches and poses can bring immediate

Since virtually any physical activity can boost mental health, your options are wide open.

benefits to a stressed or anxious person. Poses that involve sitting or lying on the floor, such as the butterfly pose or happy baby pose, are particularly beneficial. Some yoga experts say that floor poses create the feeling of being held by the earth, which can be reassuring to someone feeling unanchored by anxiety.

The martial arts of tai chi and qigong may also help reduce anxiety. Although few clinical studies have measured the impact of these ancient practices on anxiety, centuries of practitioners and students attest to their beneficial effects. Like yoga, these martial arts focus on the mind-body connection through gentle movements and mindful breathing, which help relax the nervous system.

When starting a new physical activity, do not be discouraged if you do not notice changes to your mood or anxiety levels immediately. Sixteen-year-old Laura joined a running group hoping to reduce her anxiety and depression. Although she was reluctant at the start, she eventually realized that running made her feel better. "The strategies you use in life can be used in running and vice versa," she says. "It helps me keep going instead of giving up."[19]

The Gut-Mood Connection

Food plays an essential role in mental health, although you may not realize it. After all, your parents probably encouraged you to eat your veggies to grow a healthy body, not a healthy mind! But there is no doubt that eating the right foods can have a positive impact on your psychological state and emotions. To understand why, here is a quick biology lesson.

Your brain, mood, and gastrointestinal (GI) tract have a close relationship—an unsurprising fact when you think about it. You may have felt nauseous before going on stage or get a stomachache thinking about the obnoxious bully at the park. These feelings occur because the GI tract has its own nervous system called the enteric nervous system. This system is in constant communication with the brain. When the brain tells your body to feel anxious, the enteric nervous system reacts in ways that cause disturbances in your gut as well as your emotions.

Are You Overscheduled?

Many US teens are under pressure not only to study hard but also to participate in numerous extracurricular activities. Although studies show that teens who are involved in extracurricular activities have less depression and anxiety than those who are not, having too many activities—plus a heavy course load—can negatively impact a teen's physical and mental health. "Instead of getting much needed sleep every night to recharge for the next day, teens stay up late trying to finish homework and study for tests," says psychologist Jenifer Goldman. "Even the most capable high-achievers begin to crumble under the pressure."

Goldman says you might be overscheduled if

- every moment of your day is planned;
- you are not getting enough sleep;
- you feel anxious and irritable;
- your friendships are suffering; and
- you are feeling sick more often than usual.

If your busy schedule is negatively impacting your health, you will need to manage your time better. It may involve rearranging your activities to free up time. You might have to find the courage to drop an activity or a course. Talk to your parents or a guidance counselor about how your schedule affects you and potential solutions that can protect both your well-being and academic future.

Jenifer Goldman, "6 Signs Your Teen Is Over-Scheduled and Stressed," *La Concierge Psychologist* (blog). https://laconciergepsychologist.com.

So, how does healthy eating come into play? The enteric nervous system is home to billions of so-called good bacteria that help produce neurotransmitters. One of the primary neurotransmitters is serotonin, a chemical that helps regulate mood and sleep; serotonin's presence in the body is strongly linked to decreased anxiety and depression. Scientists believe that eating certain foods encourages the growth of good bacteria, which in turn synthesizes serotonin and other feel-good neurotransmitters.

Researchers have their eye on the influence of prebiotic and probiotic foods on mental health. Probiotics are live yeasts and good bacteria that live in the body but are also found in fermented foods such as yogurt, sauerkraut, kimchi, miso, kefir, and kombucha. Prebiotics are indigestible plant fibers that serve as a food source for good bacteria. These are typically found in many fruits and vegetables, including bananas, yams, and asparagus. Several studies have found that consuming probiotic and prebiotic foods can relieve or reduce anxiety and depression symptoms.

A diet rich in vegetables, whole grains, fruit, seafood, and lean red meat has also been shown to significantly reduce anxiety and depression. As Dr. Felice Jacka, director of the Food & Mood Center at Deakin University in Australia, observes, "Eating a salad is not going to cure depression. But there's a lot you can do to lift your mood and improve your mental health, and it can be as simple as increasing your intake of plants and healthy foods."[20]

Making Healthy Food Choices

It is one thing to know we need to eat healthily, but it is another to do it. Teens and adults alike tend to gravitate toward sweet or fatty, low-nutrient foods when stressed or anxious. Studies show that calorie-dense foods such as fats and carbs stimulate the dopamine receptors in the brain's reward center, muting the body's stress response. Teens are particularly prone to fall under the spell of the reward center's response to junk food because the prefrontal cortex—the area of the brain in charge of impulse control—has not yet fully developed.

Still, there are ways to override your impulsive brain and incorporate healthier foods into your diet. Just as mindful thinking can help reduce anxiety, so can eating mindfully. Eating mindfully means being fully attuned to the food you eat, from consciously selecting foods to noticing how the food looks, smells, and tastes as you consume it to considering how the food makes you feel after you have eaten. When you eat mindfully, "you're really thinking about your values and why it's important for you personally to eat healthily,"[21] points out dietitian Maxine Smith. If you aim to diminish stress and anxiety, resolve to mindfully look for and consume healthy foods as much as possible.

Start by getting into the habit of reaching for foods containing nutrients that help relieve anxiety and stress. For example, salmon and sardines usually top the list of anxiety-busting foods because they contain vitamin D and omega-3 fatty acids. These nutrients regulate dopamine and serotonin and are linked to reduced rates of anxiety. Omega-3 also has been shown to lower inflammation in the body, which may also decrease depression and anxiety. If you are not a salmon fan, you can get similar benefits from other oily fish such as mackerel, tuna, or trout. Walnuts, eggs, flax seeds, and pumpkin seeds are also high in Omega-3s.

Look for foods containing tryptophan as well. Tryptophan is an essential amino acid crucial to the production of serotonin. You can find significant amounts of tryptophan in chicken and turkey, whole milk, canned tuna, steel-cut oats, bananas, and nuts, mainly cashews, pistachios, and almonds.

Another anxiety-reducing move would be opting for whole grains instead of processed ones. This means choosing foods such as brown rice, quinoa, popcorn, corn tortillas, whole-wheat bread, and whole oats instead of white rice, instant oatmeal, and bread products based on white flour. Whole grains are better for you than processed grains because they retain all parts of the seed, which contains a range of healthful nutrients, including anxiety-calming ones such as tryptophan and magnesium.

Naturally, fruits and vegetables are essential to any healthy diet. For anxiety reduction, Harvard Health recommends going for leafy greens such as spinach, kale, collard greens, or Swiss chard, as all are rich in magnesium. Citruses are a great antianxiety fruit choice, largely because of their high antioxidant content (one study showed that just sniffing citruses can lower anxiety). Blueberries, however, may take the top prize. Several small stud-

Because it's rich in vitamin D and Omega-3 fatty acids, salmon is one food that helps reduce anxiety and stress.

ies have indicated that a cup or two of blueberries can help decrease anxiety and depression thanks to anthocyanin, the powerful antioxidant that gives blueberries their deep blue hue.

Do not forget to drink the right beverages, too. Herbal tea is known to soothe the nerves and promote feelings of relaxation and well-being. Dietitian Amy Shapiro says in *Eat This, Not That* that peppermint tea is her top choice when she is feeling stressed, as the menthol is a natural muscle relaxant. Chamomile tea is also a classic relaxing go-to: it contains apigenin, a compound that has the same effect as certain antianxiety medications.

Not into tea? Just drink water. A 2018 study published in the *World Journal of Psychiatry* found that people who drink at least five cups of water daily have a lower risk of depression and anxiety. By contrast, those who drank fewer than two cups of water daily were twice as likely to have a negative mental state.

Tips for Eating Healthier

It can be difficult to get enthusiastic about healthy eating when you cannot stop thinking about all the unhealthy foods that you enjoy. That is why many dietitians urge people to focus on adding healthy foods to their diets instead of drastically cutting out all the bad ones. "Your diet does not need to be perfect," says dietitian Elizabeth Ward and author of the nutrition blog *Better Is the New Perfect*. "Guilt robs you of the pleasure of eating and makes you feel bad afterward, which can start a downward spiral of shame that prevents you from learning to make better eating choices while allowing for treats."

There are endless ways to incorporate more healthy foods into your diet. Start your day with a homemade blueberry-banana smoothie with a handful of fresh spinach (the sweetness of the banana masks the taste). Order pizza topped with vegetables instead of meat. Try healthier takes on favorite foods, such as salmon tacos or black bean burgers. Vow to eat a fruit or vegetable of a different color every day of the week until you have eaten the whole rainbow. Do not beat yourself up if you eat something nonnutritious—but do feel good about yourself when you eat something healthy.

Quoted in Ellie Krieger, "There's No Such Thing as Bad Food: 4 Food Terms That Make Dietitians Cringe," *Washington Post*, June 5, 2019. www.washingtonpost.com.

Sleep Well

Chloe Mauvais was just ending her sophomore year of high school when she experienced a frightening panic attack. She recalls sitting on the living room floor, crying, struggling to breathe, and feeling as if she had reached her breaking point. She was stressed and anxious about her grades and school pressures, but all those feelings were amplified by her lack of sleep. "The lack of sleep rendered me emotionally useless," she says. "I couldn't address the stress because I had no coherent thoughts. I couldn't step back and have perspective."[22]

Most US teens today are badly sleep deprived. According to the American Academy of Sleep Medicine, teens need eight to ten hours of sleep a night. However, the average high schooler gets six and a half hours of sleep a night, and one in five teens only gets five or fewer hours of sleep per night. This deficiency should not to be taken lightly.

Sleep deprivation can create a vicious cycle of increased anxiety, poor concentration, dropping grades, impaired decision-making, and negative consequences, leading to more anxiety and sleep loss. Recent studies show that lack of sleep can even lead to an uptick in suicidal thoughts.

Teen sleep deprivation is due to many factors, including early school start times, heavy homework loads, and late-night screen time. Teenagers also experience a change in their circadian rhythm, known as delayed sleep phase syndrome. This shift makes teens want to fall asleep later at night and sleep later in the mornings, a rhythm that is usually incompatible with their school schedules. "This generation of teens is the most sleep-deprived population in human history," write Heather Turgeon and Julie Wright, authors of *Generation Sleepless*. "Imagine an experiment in which researchers forced subjects to wake up three hours before their natural rise time, then asked them to perform complex cognitive tasks, for five days straight. That's a description of the average teen's school week."[23]

Taking Control of Sleep

Take control of your sleep situation by developing a consistent sleep routine. To get started, therapist Amy Morin suggests finding your ideal bedtime, which is the time you need to get up for school minus nine hours. If you have to rise by 7 a.m., your ideal bedtime would be 10 p.m. You do not necessarily have to be asleep by the target hour, but it should mark the start of a quiet time that tells your brain to calm down and prepare for sleep.

Make a list of peaceful activities that would help you fall asleep and incorporate them into your bedtime routine.

> "This generation of teens is the most sleep-deprived population in human history."[23]
>
> —Heather Turgeon and Julie Wright, authors of *Generation Sleepless*

Typical winding-down activities include playing soothing music, taking a warm bath or shower, meditating, or drinking warm milk or a sleep-inducing herbal tea, such as lavender or chamomile. Twelve-year-old Josephine found she slept much better and was less anxious after performing simple yoga breathing and stretching routines before bed. She also began wearing a sleep mask for total darkness and ditched one of her favorite activities—reading in bed—which kept her brain too active.

Be careful to avoid anxiety triggers before bedtime. That means turning off the news, social media, scary movies, or anything else that heightens your anxiety well before you hit the sheets. If anxious thoughts persist, consider creating a sleep journal in which you write down all your anxieties and worries. Many sleep experts say that when you take worrying thoughts from your head and

Experts say that teens need eight to ten hours of sleep per night. Developing a consistent sleep routine is an important first step in getting enough rest.

put them on paper before bedtime, they are more likely to stay there when you go to sleep. In 2018, a small study at Baylor University found that when students wrote down their next-day to-do lists before going to bed, they fell asleep faster than students who did not.

Sleep experts are adamant that all screens—whether video, gaming, cell phones, or computer—must be turned off at least an hour before bedtime. Not only does engaging with these devices keep your brain in an excitable state, but electronic screens also emit blue light. This wavelength of light suppresses the production of melatonin, a hormone instrumental in helping you fall asleep. If you need to use a computer for schoolwork, try to do the online work as early in the evening as possible, and save the off-screen work for later.

CHAPTER FOUR

Healing Anxiety

Katy has had social anxiety since she was young. She hated doing anything that made her stand out and was afraid of looking bad in front of others. As she grew older, she began to develop debilitating anxiety attacks in social situations. It was only when she examined and understood the root cause of her anxiety that she started to take control of the attacks. "I grew up in a small town where everyone is white. I'm not. My father is black and my mother is white. I never felt like I fit in," Katy says. "I always felt like I was different or that there was something wrong with me. I know now that this was a fear of judgment."[24]

Katy realized she had learned to be afraid of social situations because people had judged her in the past. Once she understood the source of the fear controlling her, she began focusing on loving and accepting herself and stopped looking at herself through the eyes of others. Now a social anxiety coach herself, Katy firmly believes that knowing what caused her social anxiety was a crucial first step in healing.

As Katy learned, you can heal from anxiety, even if you are never completely cured. Because anxiety is a natural stress response, no one can or should completely eliminate it. However, you can take steps to shrink it to a manageable size. Then you can begin to live the life you really want.

Identify the Source of Your Anxiety

Anxiety can develop for all kinds of reasons. You might have experienced a traumatic, stressful, or scary situation in your past, and now your anxious brain is triggered by any mental associations with that event. It could also come from a medical condition or certain medications. You could be drinking too much caffeine or gorging on junk food. There is even some evidence that anxiety can be passed genetically.

With so many potential sources, it is not easy to figure out the root of your anxiety. You may need a mental health professional or medical doctor to help, and even then, there may not be a clear answer. But sometimes, sitting with your anxiety and conducting your own investigation can bring about an important revelation.

Chantal McCulligh, founder of the mental health blog *Anxiety Gone*, recommends getting to the root of your feelings by asking yourself several questions during or after an anxious moment:

- What am I feeling?
- Why am I feeling this?
- What has changed in my life in the last two months, six months, or year?
- Are there other times in my life where I felt the same way, albeit in a different situation?
- Is there a common thread here?[25]

Your answers to these questions might reveal events, experiences, or patterns that you previously had not connected to your anxiety. You may not find the answer right away, but keeping track of your responses in an anxiety journal can help you connect the dots and see the bigger picture over time.

McCulligh warns not to mistake an anxiety trigger as the root of anxiety. For instance, school might trigger your anxiety, but the specific reason why school makes you anxious is the root cause. After reflecting, you might realize that school makes you anxious

Keeping an anxiety journal is one way of getting at the root of your feelings.

because your math teacher cold-calls on students, which reminds you of a bad experience with cold-calling when you froze up. Or you are anxious because you think other students are laughing at you when you pass them in the hall. Or you fear you will be scolded by a teacher (again) because you have difficulty paying attention in class. When you break down the source of anxiety to that level, you might be able to identify the issues that need resolving.

Look for Solutions

You might not be able to solve every problem entirely, but you might find solutions that are good enough to lessen your anxiety or make you feel more in control. Youth Era, a group dedicated to empowering youth, recommends a three-step process for finding solutions. First, define the problem as precisely as possible. Next, brainstorm as many creative solutions as possible, no matter how far-fetched, and weigh the pros and cons of each. Finally, decide on a realistic, rational approach that is most likely to yield the best outcome for you.

To use the cold-calling math teacher as an example, here are three possible brainstormed solutions: 1) never going to math class again, 2) studying math like crazy to always be prepared, and 3) talking to the teacher about how to reduce your anxiety in class. In the pros and cons stage, you may decide that skipping math sounds good, but it is not realistic and will create more problems. Pouring all your energy into preparing for class may help, but it would also be exhausting, and you might freeze up when called on anyway. Talking to the teacher might be a little scary, but maybe she has worked with anxious students before and would have some good suggestions. In this instance, the third idea might produce the best outcome for you.

Do not hesitate to discuss potential solutions with others, whether parents, friends, or a teacher. High schooler Natalie Castelan realized she needed to find a solution to her anxiety after she froze and could not speak during a class presentation in her freshman year. She dreaded all presentations afterwards and stuttered her way through them, feeling miserable. In tenth grade, she decided to write a letter to her English teacher, explaining her anxiety and other problems she was facing.

After reading the letter, Natalie's teacher shared that she, too, suffered from anxiety. Natalie ended up talking to a school counselor, who helped her gain confidence with breathing exercises and other tips. Natalie says, "This year, we had to give another group presentation like the one on that awful day when I was a freshman. When it came to my part, all my fears went away, and I spoke loud and proud."[26]

Face Your Fears

For many teens, avoiding anxiety-triggering situations seems the best solution to getting around anxiety. Instead of walking down

Many teens feel anxious about tests. One way to reduce anxiety and build confidence is to visualize, or mentally rehearse, taking the test—and doing well.

the hall where you would have to pass certain students who make you anxious, you take a different route, even though it is longer and more inconvenient. But therapists say that avoiding anxious situations makes your anxiety worse, not better. "[Avoidance] tells our brains that there's a valid reason to be anxious, even if there isn't,"[27] explains Jessica Frick, a licensed counselor.

Facing your fears can be frightening but empowering. When Marie-Therese began having panic attacks in eighth grade, she refused to go to school for weeks. Her parents sent her to a psychologist, where she learned how to cope with the attacks through muscle relaxation and breathing exercises. Eventually, she returned to school with permission to leave the classroom if she felt an attack coming on.

Although Marie-Therese's friends supported her return, some popular kids made a game of doing disturbing things, such as staring at her with their eyelids turned inside out, to try to make her leave the room. The bullying made her so angry that she forced herself to stay in her seat, refusing to give in to panic. Bit by bit, she gained control over the attacks. By the end of the year, she even won a school talent show by playing the piano. "I felt so proud of myself, not because I'd won, but because I'd beaten the panic attacks."[28]

There are many ways to face your fears. Some experts recommend starting with confronting your fear through a technique called mental rehearsal or visualization. Studies have shown that mentally rehearsing how you would handle a difficult or stressful scenario can help you achieve a positive outcome in real-life situations.

Developing Self-Compassion

People with anxiety tend to judge themselves harshly, especially teens. Psychologists say that teens can spend too much time dwelling on mistakes, faulty perceptions of themselves, or believing that others are as attentive to them as they are to themselves. Such self-scrutiny can result in severe self-assessments. "The need for self-compassion among teens is paramount," says Karen Bluth, a psychologist who teaches a course for teens called Mindful Self-Compassion for Teens. "Sad to say, almost 80 percent of us treat others with more compassion and kindness than we offer to ourselves."

When you are feeling bad about yourself and anxiety is taking over, treat yourself as you would treat someone you love who is going through a bad time:

- Write yourself a loving letter, describing all the beautiful things about you, as if you were your best friend.
- Write down all negative self-talk you say and look at it objectively: do you deserve to be spoken to this way? Most of the time, you will realize that you do not.
- Forgive your mistakes: no one gets away with a mistake-free life, including you.
- Hug yourself or stroke your cheek. Bluth says your own touch can lower your stress and make you feel better.

Karen Bluth, "How to Help Teens Become More Self-Compassionate," *Greater Good Magazine*, October 19, 2017. https://greatergood.berkeley.edu.

The technique is famous among athletes, such as basketball player LeBron James, who spends a few moments visualizing himself performing well before every game. Brett Steenbarger, a psychologist who advocates mental rehearsals, says, "It doesn't matter what the problem is. . . . We can vividly evoke those experiences, shift our state, reframe the situation, and rehearse desired actions. When we do this again and again, we build novel brain pathways and new, positive habit patterns."[29]

To mentally rehearse, get comfortable in a safe, peaceful space, then visualize an anxiety-triggering scenario. As your anxiety rises, visualize yourself handling the entire situation as you would want it to happen. For example, if you are anxious about taking a test, imagine walking into the classroom, sitting down, and taking out a pen or doing whatever you would ordinarily do. Engage all your senses: imagine what the classroom smells like, hear the chatter of the other students around you, feel the pen in your hand. Even allow yourself to feel your anxiety as you wait for your teacher to start passing the tests around.

Then, imagine how you would like this scenario to ideally unfold. See yourself breathing evenly as you look at the test and feel your confidence building as you write answers. You can even imagine encountering a tricky question and calmly skipping it to return to it later or working through it without getting frustrated. Picture having time to review the exam before handing it in and then feel your relief and excitement that it is over. You should always feel like an active participant in the scenario, not a passive observer.

The more you mentally rehearse capably handling an anxious scenario, the more confident and less anxious you will be when encountering that situation in real life. Repetition is key. "You are creating new associations in your mind and that can take time," says therapist Deborah Winyard. "Remember you spent a long time in the past practicing and becoming superb at being anxious. . . . It may take a little while to install your new habit of being calm and confident."[30]

Affirmations for Anxiety

Affirmations are short positive statements intended to help you overcome negative thinking or a stressful situation. Repeating positive affirmations regularly can change your thought patterns—and even some neural pathways. "There's a really cool brain basis for these self-affirmation effects," says psychologist David Creswell, a professor at Carnegie Mellon University. "They're really turning on the brain's reward system, and that reward system [muffles] your stress alarm system in ways that can be helpful."

When you feel anxiety rising or negativity taking over your thoughts, try repeating one of the following affirmations for two or three minutes. Even if you do not quite believe the words, repeat them as if you do. Eventually your mind will catch up. For best results, develop the habit of saying affirmations daily, even if you are not anxious at that moment.

"I am safe. Right here, right now."
"This moment will pass."
"I release the past and embrace the present."
"I have handled anxiety before. I can handle it now."
"I forgive myself."
"I love myself and that is enough."
"I do the best I can and that is enough."
"I am in charge of me."
"I choose to feel calm."

Quoted in Allyson Chiu, "How to Make Self-Affirmation Work, Based on Science." *Washington Post*, May 2, 2022. www.washingtonpost.com.

Another way of facing your fears is using positive self-talk. Just as it sounds, positive self-talk is talking to yourself positively or encouragingly. Everyone talks to themselves, but we often do not realize how many negative things we say and how badly these words can impact our mental health. Positive self-talk counters negativity and helps us to think in a healthier, more positive, and rational way.

Engage in positive self-talk by catching fearful thoughts and reframing them in a positive light. For instance, if you become anxious while studying and think, *I'm so dumb, I'll never pass this exam*, you could replace that thought with, *I've never actually failed an exam before, this one will be fine too*, or *No matter what happens, I'll still be okay*. Fifteen-year-old Mehek Azra, who uses positive self-talk to get through challenging moments of social anxiety, offers this advice:

> Talk to yourself the way you wish others would talk to you. Never disrespect yourself. Remind yourself that as much as you may think others are judging you, most of the time they are just busy with themselves. The teenagers in the mall laughed because one of their friends made a joke. That one girl laughed when you were reading out loud because she and her friend were making inside jokes that did not involve you. We stress too much about how others see us. But you need to see yourself for who you are.[31]

> "Talk to yourself the way you wish others would talk to you. Never disrespect yourself."[31]
>
> —Mehek Azra, a fifteen-year-old student with social anxiety

You can also face your fear by putting it in perspective. Imagine an anxiety-triggering moment and ask yourself two questions: 1) What is the worst that could happen? 2) Could you survive the consequences if it occurs? You probably can. You may feel shattered if you fail an exam or humiliate yourself on the volleyball court, but you can survive it. Maybe you will even learn an important lesson: people can bounce back after terrible things happen. This ability to rebound is called resilience.

Some teens have been surprised to discover their resiliency after their worst fears came true. Morgan, a college student, worked to exhaustion from sixth grade to senior year, hoping to get into Columbia University, where five generations of family had attended. Morgan was devastated at not being accepted but soon saw an unexpected upside. "I felt free for the first time in my life," Morgan says. "I am now a sophomore at a college that I love and belong at."[32]

Help Others

There is no denying that we live in anxious times. Stories of political strife, climate change, war, violence, and societal inequities dominate the news cycles. It is hard to remain emotionally unaffected by such events, especially if you are a teen about to step into the world. If negativity in the world is fueling your anxiety, the best antidote may be to add positivity.

"There is a lot of evidence that one of the best anti-anxiety medications available is generosity,"[33] says psychologist Adam Grant. Research shows that volunteering can increase dopamine and lower cortisol levels. It can also foster confidence, self-esteem, and social connections as well as give you a sense of purpose. The positive mental boost people receive from helping others is so strong that some researchers have called on mental health professionals to include volunteering as part of clinical treatment for depressed adolescents.

> "There is a lot of evidence that one of the best anti-anxiety medications available is generosity."[33]
>
> —Adam Grant, a psychologist and author

You do not have to become the next Greta Thunberg, however, to make the world a better place. Preparing a meal in a local soup kitchen; donating food, clothing, or supplies to a homeless shelter; helping a needy child with homework; giving a homeless person warm socks; or grocery shopping for an elderly neighbor are all small acts of kindness that can make you and others feel great. Look around your community and consider how you might be able to improve it in some way or identify vulnerable people or groups that could use your help.

If a larger social or global concern keeps you up at night, consider ways you can make a difference. It could be as simple as picking litter off the beach every Saturday or as complex as working with an organization or politicians to fight for a specific cause. Sixteen-year-old Madigan Traversi, who suffered from anxiety after losing her home in a California wildfire, now channels her

Helping others is a good way of giving yourself a mental boost. Preparing meals at a local soup kitchen or donating food, clothing, or supplies to a homeless shelter are some of the many ways to help make the world a better place.

fears into fighting climate change. She is the coleader of Schools for Climate Action, a nonprofit organization dedicated to working with Congress to act on climate issues, and has even helped author a bill focused on the mental health impact of climate-related disasters on youth.

Blogging or vlogging about an issue you care about is another way to help others and soothe your own emotions. Blogger Sean Clarke found his anxiety receded when he achieved his goal to help people by creating a mental health website, the kind that did not exist when he was an anxious teen.

Accept Anxiety

Accepting anxiety is one of the most important actions you can take to heal from it. The more you see anxiety as a normal part of your life, the less power it will have over you. This idea may seem contradictory or ironic, but your frustration or anger at having anxiety helps feed it. You become anxious about being anxious.

Accepting anxiety means different things to different people. For some, it means learning to live with it. It means having and using an arsenal of coping skills when anxiety rears. It means seeking help and support from friends, family, teachers, therapists, or doctors or using prescribed medication when needed. But you accept this as part of your life. "Accepting anxiety into your life is like accepting that it might rain when you're trying to throw a garden party. It can just happen," says Clarke. "Instead of fighting [anxiety] with every inch of strength I have, I now try to observe it as it is, a passing emotion that does not define me as a person."[34]

Other mental health experts, such as counselor Jodi Lobozzo Aman, encourage people to accept anxiety like an acquaintance who has stopped by. Ask it why it has come—is there an issue that needs addressing? Do you need more sleep or to get started on the English assignment you have been avoiding? If anxiety is trying to tell you something, thank it for the heads-up and start considering how you can resolve the problem.

However, if anxiety has come for no identifiable reason, then you know it does not require your attention. Aman recommends simply accepting its presence without judgment or fear and trying not to let it derail you from whatever you are doing, as it wants to do. Just say to it, *"Hello, I knew you'd come back. . . . Have a seat, I am painting right now."*[35] And continue with your life.

SOURCE NOTES

Introduction: Youth in Distress

1. Brynn, "Overcoming Teen Depression and Anxiety: Brynn's Story," *Phoenix Family Center Blog*, August 18, 2018. http://phoenixfamilycenter.com.
2. Brynn, "Overcoming Teen Depression and Anxiety."
3. Vivek Murthy, introduction to *Protecting Youth Mental Health: The U.S. Surgeon General's Advisory*, by the Office of the Surgeon General. Washington, DC: US Department of Health and Human Services, 2021. www.hhs.gov.
4. Quoted in Learning Network Staff, "What It's Like to Be a Teenager Now: The Winners of Our Coming of Age in 2021 Contest," *New York Times*, January 5, 2022. www.nytimes.com.
5. Quoted in Jennifer Gunn, "Why Anxiety Is So Prevalent in Teens and What Can be Done," Resilient Educator. https://resilienteducator.com.

Chapter One: Recognizing Anxiety

6. Christi Cazin, "I Didn't Know I Had Anxiety Until I Was 31," Romper, August 13, 2016. www.romper.com.
7. Charlotte Lieberman, "How to Manage Your Anxiety," *Harvard Business Review*, September 2020. https://hbr.org.
8. Tyler Ellis, "My First Panic Attack to My Last," Anxiety Resource Center, August 2021. www.anxietyresourcecenter.org.
9. Quoted in Caroline Miller, "Mental Health Disorders and Teen Substance Abuse," Child Mind Institute, July 28, 2022. https://childmind.org.
10. Quoted in Susanna Schrobsdorff, "Teen Depression and Anxiety: Why the Kids Are Not Alright," *Time*, November 7, 2016. https://time.com.

11. Katie Hurley, "How to Tell Your Parents You Need Help," Psycom, February 3, 2022. www.psycom.net.

Chapter Two: Get Grounded, Stay Connected

12. Kerry, "The Grounding Technique That Helps Me When I'm Anxious," *Young Minds* (blog), October 19, 2020. www.youngminds.org.uk.
13. Molly, "Struggling with Anxiety as a Teenager: Molly's Story," *Anxiety Gone* (blog), August 3, 2018. https://anxiety-gone.com.
14. Kerry, "The Grounding Technique That Helps Me When I'm Anxious."
15. Quoted in Kathleen Ferraro, "7 Ways Music Can Help Reduce Stress and Anxiety," American Society of Composers, Authors, and Publishers, September 10, 2021. www.ascap.com.
16. Quoted in Kimberly Truong, "Here's Why Venting About Stress Feels So Good," Refinery 29, August 23, 2018. www.refinery29.com.

Chapter Three: Maintain a Healthy Lifestyle

17. Quoted in BBC News, "Newcastle Teen Combats Anxiety with Exercise," video, June 11, 2019. www.bbc.com.
18. Quoted in Perri Klass, "The Benefit of Exercise for Children's Mental Health*,*" *New York Times*, March 2, 2020. www.nytimes.com.
19. Quoted in Kate Daley, "Teen Mental Health: The Benefits of Running," *Canadian Living*, August 25, 2014. www.canadianliving.com.
20. Quoted in Anahad O'Connor, "How Food May Improve Your Mood," *New York Times*, December 21, 2021. www.nytimes.com.
21. Quoted in Cleveland Clinic, "Mindful Eating," January 31, 2022. https://health.clevelandclinic.org.
22. Quoted in Ruthanne Richter, "Among Teens, Sleep Deprivation an Epidemic," Stanford Medicine News Center, October 8, 2015. https://med.stanford.edu.

23. Heather Turgeon and Julie Wright, "We're Ignoring a Major Culprit Behind the Mental Health Crisis," *Washington Post*, May 20, 2022. www.washingtonpost.com.

Chapter Four: Healing Anxiety

24. Katy Morin, "I Had to Find the Root Cause of My Social Anxiety to Finally Heal," *Better Humans* (blog), August 26, 2021. https://betterhumans.pub.
25. Chantal McCulligh, "Root Causes of Anxiety and How to Find Them," *Anxiety Gone* (blog), September 24, 2020. https://anxiety-gone.com.
26. Natalie Castelan, "I was Too Anxious to Speak in Class. Then the Adults at My School Teamed Up to Help Me," Chalkbeat New York, February 20, 2019. https://ny.chalkbeat.org.
27. Quoted in Simone Scully, "The Importance of Accepting Anxiety," PsychCentral, June 5, 2022. https://psychcentral.com.
28. Marie-Therese Miller, "Panic," in *Chicken Soup for the Soul: Teens Talk Tough Times: Stories about the Hardest Parts of Being a Teenager*, ed. Jack Canfield et al. New York: Simon & Schuster, 2009, p. 23.
29. Brett Steenbarger, "Tapping the Power of Mental Rehearsals," *Forbes*, February 17, 2018. www.forbes.com.
30. Deborah Winyard, "Scared of Tests? A 4-Step Process to Help You Overcome Your Fears," *Deborah Winyard Hypnotherapy Blog*, April 29, 2018. www.deborahwinyardhypnotherapy.com.
31. Mehek Azra, "What It's Like to Be a Teen with Social Anxiety," *Skipping Stones* (blog), March 23, 2021. www.skippingstones.org.
32. Quoted in Alice Yin, "Coping with Teenage Anxiety: Readers Share Their Stories," *New York Times*, October 23, 2017. www.nytimes.com.
33. Quoted in Tara Parker-Pope, "The Science of Helping Out," *New York Times*, April 9, 2020. www.nytimes.com.
34. Sean Clarke, "Accepting Anxiety into My Life Has Taken Away Its Power over Me," *No Panic* (blog), https://nopanic.org.uk.
35. Jodi Lobozzo Amam, "What Do Accepting and Letting Go of Anxiety Mean?," *Healthy Place* (blog), September 18, 2013. www.healthyplace.com.

ORGANIZATIONS AND WEBSITES

American Academy of Child & Adolescent Psychiatry (AACAP)

www.aacap.org

The AACAP educates the public about health issues affecting children and teens. Its website has ample information about how youth and their parents can cope with anxiety and anxiety disorder.

American Psychological Association (APA)

www.apa.org

The APA is dedicated to informing the public about psychology and its relevance to society and individual lives. Its website has a section devoted to anxiety disorders and features numerous articles about anxiety and how to live with it.

Anxiety and Depression Association of America (ADAA)

www.adaa.org

The ADAA is an organization dedicated to preventing, treating, and curing anxiety disorders and depression. It discusses all aspects of anxiety, including how to manage stress and anxiety, and it offers online support groups.

Child Mind Institute

www.childmind.org

The Child Mind Institute is dedicated to transforming the lives of children, adolescents, and families struggling with mental health issues. It provides a range of articles and information about anxiety on its website, including information about anxiety and social media.

National Social Anxiety Center
https://nationalsocialanxietycenter.com
The National Social Anxiety Center is committed to bringing greater awareness and understanding of social anxiety to the public. The site offers numerous resources to those in need, including articles, self-help videos, audio recordings of sample therapy sessions, and a blog.

988 Suicide and Crisis Lifeline
988 has been designated as the new three-digit dialing code that will route callers to the National Suicide Prevention Lifeline. When people call, text, or chat 988, they will be connected to trained counselors who will listen, provide support, and connect them to any needed resources. Counselors are available twenty-four hours a day, seven days a week.

Teen Health 101
www.teenhealth101.org
Teen Health 101 is a youth-led nonprofit organization that focuses on providing simple yet accurate health information to youth. The site discusses and offers tips on improving both physical and mental health, including dealing with anxiety.

FOR FURTHER RESEARCH

Books

Tabatha Chansard, *Conquer Anxiety Workbook for Teens: Find Peace from Worry, Panic, Fear, and Phobias*. Emeryville, CA: Althea, 2019.

Natasha Daniels, *Anxiety Sucks! A Teen Survival Guide*. Scotts Valley, CA: CreateSpace Independent Publishing Platform, 2016.

Regine Galanti, *Anxiety Relief for Teens: Essential CBT Skills and Mindfulness Practices to Overcome Anxiety and Stress*. New York: Penguin Random House, 2020.

Debra Kissin et al., *Rewire Your Anxious Brain for Teens: Using CBT, Neuroscience, and Mindfulness to Help You End Anxiety, Panic, and Worry*. Oakland, CA: Instant Help, 2020.

Jamie D. Roberts, *Mindfulness for Teen Anxiety: A Practical Guide to Manage Stress, Ease Worry, and Find Calm*. Oakland, CA: Rockridge, 2022.

Barbara Sheen, *Teen Guide to Managing Stress and Anxiety*. San Diego: ReferencePoint, 2022.

Internet Sources

Gopala Amir-Yaffe, "10 Cool Meditations for PreTeens and Teens," DoYou, March 5, 2021. www.doyou.com.

Sheryl Ankrom, "9 Breathing Exercises to Relieve Anxiety," VeryWell Mind, August 24, 2022. www.verywellmind.com.

Dasia Bandy, "How to Help Teens Guide Their Friends in Need of Mental Health Resources," *Parents*, August 2, 2022. www.parents.com.

Brittney McNamara, "How to Handle Four Anxiety Causes," *Teen Vogue*, September 14, 2017. www.teenvogue.com.

Uma Naidoo, "Nutritional Strategies to Ease Anxiety," *Mind & Mood* (blog), Harvard Health, August 29, 2019. www.health.harvard.edu.

Optimist Daily, "5 Ways a Neuroscientist Turns Anxiety into Productive Energy," November 10, 2021. www.optimistdaily.com.

Matt Richtel, "'It's Life or Death:' The Mental Health Crisis Among U.S. Teens," *New York Times*, May 3, 2022. www.nytimes.com.

Derek Thompson, "Why American Teens Are So Sad," *Atlantic*, April 11, 2022. www.theatlantic.com.

INDEX

Note: Boldface page numbers indicate illustrations.

addiction, 15–16
adolescents. *See* teens
adrenaline, 14–15
affirmations, 49
alphabet game, 23
Aman, Jodi Lobozzo, 53
American Academy of Pediatrics, 5
American Academy of Sleep Medicine, 38
animals and grounding, 23
anxiety
  controlling and healing
    by accepting as normal part of life, 10, 52–53
    brainstorming solutions for, 44–45, **46**
    by developing self-compassion, 47
    by grounding. *See* grounding anxiety
    helping others and, 51–52, **52**
    putting fears in perspective and, 50
    by using positive self-talk, 49–50
    by using visualization, 48
  disorder and brain, 10–11
  fight-or-flight response and, 10, 13
  identifying source of, 42–44, **44**
  recognizing, 9
  social media and, 7, 25–26
  stress hormones and, 14–15
  symptoms of, 4, 12
    behavioral and emotional, 13–14, 19
    fight-or-flight response as, 10
    out-of-body sensation as, 21
    physical, 12
    psychological, 12–13
  worry as cognitive component of, 13
Anxiety Gone (blog), 32
Ashton, Chloe, 26
Azra, Mehek, 50

Baylor University, 41
belly breathing, 20–21
Better Is the New Perfect (blog), 38

Black youth and mental health crises risks, 5–6, **6**
blueberries, 36–37
Bluth, Karen, 47
body image and use of Instagram, 7
box breathing, 20
brain
  action of, upon detecting danger or stress, 10, **11**
  amygdala, 27–28
  anxiety disorder and, 10–11
  dopamine released by
    calorie-dense foods and, 35
    helping others and, 51
    music and, 24
    pets and, 23
    regulation of, 36
  exercise and, 30–31
  music and, 24–25
  prefrontal cortex development, 16, 35
  self-affirmations and, 49
  serotonin released by, 23, 36
  yoga and, 32
breathing techniques, 20–21, **21**, 24

Castelan, Natalie, 45
Cazin, Christi, 9
Centers for Disease Control and Prevention (CDC), 5, 31
Clarke, Sean, 52, 53
Common Sense Media, 25
cortisol, 14–15, 51
COVID-19 pandemic, 5, 7, 17
Creswell, David, 49
Cyberpsychology, Behaviour and Social Networking (journal), 25–26

Davis, Amelia, 16
deep breathing, 20, **21**, 24
delayed sleep phase syndrome, 39
dopamine
  calorie-dense foods and, 35
  helping others and, 51
  music and, 24
  pets and, 23
  regulation of, 36
Duffy, Courtney, 7

eating disorders, 4, 16
eating habits, 35–38, **37**
Eat This, Not That (Shapiro), 37
Ellis, Tyler, 12
emotions, naming, 27–29
Environment and Behavior (magazine), 23
exercise, 30–33, **32**

Facebook, 7
FAIR Health, 17
fight-or-flight response
    activation of, 15
    anxiety and, 10, 13
    described, 10, **11**
    hormones produced by, 14
    stress and, 13
5-4-3-2-1 grounding technique, 23
fluids, 37
FOMO (fear of missing out), 7
food, 35–38, **37**
Frick, Jessica, 46

Game Quitters, 26
gaming, 26
gamma-aminobutyric acid (GABA), 32
gender
    exercise and, 31
    suicide attempts by, 5
    self-harm and, 16
    social media and depression by, 7
generalized anxiety disorder (GAD), 11
Generation Sleepless (Turgeon and Wright), 39
generosity, 51
Grant, Adam, 51
Greenberg, Melanie, 13
grounding anxiety
    basic facts about, 19
    techniques for
    animals and, 23
    breathing, 20–21, **21**
    cooking, 28
    eating habits and, 35–38, **37**
    exercise, 30–33, **32**
    internet breaks and, 25–27
    listening to music and, **24**, 24–25
    meditation, 26
    mindfulness exercises and, 22–23
    reconnecting with body and, 21–22
    talking about negative emotions and, 27–29
    use of scent of lavender and, 21

Harvard Business Review (magazine), 10
Harvard Health, 36
Healthy Children (website), 5
hopelessness, percentage of teens with persistent feelings of, 5
hormones, stress
    effects of long-term production of, 14–15
    exercise and, 31
    music and, 24–25
    produced in fight-or-flight response, 14
    See also specific hormones
How Music Can Make You Better (Viskontas), 24–25
Hurley, Katie, 18

Instagram, 7
internet breaks, 25–27

JAMA Psychiatry (journal), 25
James, LeBron, 48
Journal of the American Academy of Child and Adolescent Psychiatry, 14
journals, keeping, 27, **44**
junk food, 35

lavender, scent of, 21
Lieberman, Charlotte, 10, 12

magnesium, 36
Marques, Luana, 13
Mauvais, Chloe, 38
McCulligh, Chantal, 32
McMahon, Elaine, 31
meditation, 26
mental health crises
    emergency room visits by teens for, 5
    minorities at highest risk for, 5–6, **6**
    openness about mental health issues and, 8
    prevention hotline for, 18
Merk, Lynne, 8
Miller, Louise, 23
mindfulness
    exercises for, 22–23
    grounding and, 19
    See also grounding anxiety
Morris, Ben, 30
Murthy, Vivek, 5
music and controlling anxiety, **24**, 24–25

National Institute for Mental Health, 11
National Suicide Prevention Lifeline, 18

New York Times (newspaper), 7
988 Suicide and Crisis Lifeline, 18

obsessive-compulsive disorder, 11
omega-3 fatty acids, 36, **37**

panic attacks, 12
pets as grounding aids, 23
physical health
    exercise and mental health, 30–33, **32**
    illnesses and failure to receive treatment, 16
    long-term production of stress hormones and, 14–15
positive self-talk, 49–50
Psychology Today (magazine), 23

qigong, 33

Ringgold, Tim, 24

sadness, percentage of teens with persistent feelings of, 5
Schools for Climate Action, 52
self-affirmations, 49
self-compassion, developing, 47
self-harm, 16–17
self-medication, **14**, 15–16
serotonin, 23, 36
Shapiro, Amy, 37
Siegel, Dan, 29
sleep, 38–41, **40**
Smith, Julie, 22
Smith, Maxine, 36
social media
    anxiety and, 7, 25–26
    depression in teen girls and, 7
    sleep and, 41
square breathing, 20
Steenbarger, Brett, 48
stressors
    faced by teens today, 7
    fight-or-flight response and, 10, **11**, 13, 15
suicide
    as cause of death of teens, 17
    increase in, by teen girls, 5
    lack of sleep and, 39
    prevention hotline, 18
symptoms of anxiety, 4, 12
    behavioral and emotional, 13–14, 19
    fight-or-flight response as, 10
    out-of-body sensation as, 21
    physical, 12
    psychological, 12–13

tai chi, 33
teens
    average time on social media, 25
    emergency room visits by, 5
    exercise and, 31
    increase in suicide attempts by girls, 5
    percentage of, self-harming, 16–17
    percentage of, receiving treatment, 14
    percentage of, suffering from anxiety disorder, 11
    percentage of, with persistent feelings of sadness or hopelessness, 5
    sleep and, 38–41, **40**
    social media and depression in, 7
    suicide by, 17
Traversi, Madigan, 51–52
treatment
    asking for help and, **17**, 17–18
    coping mechanisms and, **14**, 15–16
    failure to receive, physical effects of, 14–15, 16
    percentage of teens receiving, 14
triggers
    avoiding, 45–46
    examples of, 15
    facing fears and, 46–47
    root of anxiety and, 43–44
    understanding, and coping with anxiety, 15
tryptophan, 36
Turgeon, Heather, 39
Twenge, Jean, 7

University of Georgia, 31

Viskontas, Indre, 24–25
visualization, 48
vitamin D, 36, **37**

Ward, Elizabeth, 38
water, and lower risk of anxiety, 37
Weber, Carissa, 16
Winyard, Deborah, 48
World Journal of Psychiatry, 37
worry, as cognitive component of anxiety, 13
worthlessness, feelings of, 4
Wright, Julie, 39

yoga, 32–33
youth. *See* teens
Youth Era, 44–45

Ziegler, Sheryl, 7

PICTURE CREDITS

Cover: fizkes/Shutterstock

6: fizkes/Shutterstock
11: Sciencepics/Shutterstock
14: sruilk/Shutterstock
17: True Touch Lifestyle/Shutterstock
21: Antonio Guillem/Shutterstock
24: Prostock-studio/Shutterstock
28: Fabian Ponce Garcia/Shutterstock
32: Jacek Chabraszewski/Shutterstock
37: Timolina/Shutterstock
40: wavebreakmedia/Shutterstock
44: Antonio Guillem/Shutterstock
46: Wavebreak/iStock
52: Monkey Business Images/Shutterstock